DARK CLAW

The Black Hole

May the Guiding Paw be with you!

First published in Great Britain in 2002
by Hodder Children's Books

Copyright © 2002 Shoo Rayner

10 9 8 7 6 5 4 3 2 1

The right of
Shoo Rayner to be identified as the Author of
the Work has been asserted by him in accordance with the Copyright,
Designs and Patents Act 1988.

A Catalogue record for this book is available from the
British Library

ISBN 0 340 81759 3

Printed and bound in Great Britain by
Bookmarque Ltd, Croydon, Surrey

Hodder Children's Books
a division of Hodder Headline Limited
338 Euston Road
London NW1 3BH

Chapter 1

A Rob Kat's voice crackled over the radio and Chancellor Brandling slammed on the reverse thrusters.

"Wait there!" came the Robo Kat's reply.

As she waited, the Chancellor sat fuming in her spacecraft.

Onlee One had escaped death once again and spoiled her plan to be ruler of all Muss! She could never go home… unless she could strike a deal with Dark Claw.

The Rob Kat's voice broke into her thoughts.

Dark Claw will speak with you… proceed.

Brandling smiled to herself. Now that he had agreed to see her, Dark Claw was bound to agree to her plan! The hard part of her mission was over.

She slid the control stick forward and set a course for Dark Moon.

Chapter 2

Top Muss was meeting with the Muss
Council. Before him stood a group of
nervous guards and officials. All of
them had worked for Brandling.

Now that she had deserted them, they
were certain they would be charged
with treason, just as Brandling had
been.

Top Muss spoke to them. "Dark Claw is our deadly enemy and Brandling is now in league with him. She cannot save you now. If you'll work with us to save the planet Muss from Dark Claw, you will be forgiven."

The traitors had expected to go to prison at least. They did not hesitate. "We promise!" they cried.

Top Muss looked across at Onlee One and his two friends, Hammee and Chin Chee. His mood stayed serious.

> Once again, Onlee One has saved the planet from certain danger. He and his team have risked their lives to help save our planet. We owe him our thanks.

The Council members nodded in agreement.

"But we are not out of danger yet!" Top Muss went on. "We must try harder to rid the universe of Dark Claw, for ever!"

Then he stood and swept out of the Council Chamber , beckoning all to join him in the planning room. "Come! There is very little time!"

Brandling's guards and officials followed quickly. They had already forgotten Brandling. Now there was serious work to be done.

Hammee turned to Onlee One. "I don't suppose you fancy a little snack first, do you?" he asked.

Chapter 3

Meanwhile, on Dark Claw's secret space station, Dark Moon, Brandling was explaining her plan.

> I understand your hatred of Onlee One, Dark Claw, but there is no need to destroy us all.

Dark Claw's cold expression did not change, and Brandling hesitated before going on.

"Why destroy *all* Muss…" she continued,
"…when some can be your slaves?
I will help you. I can take command
of the Muss. They respect me."

Feeling more confident, Brandling
continued. "When I give the order, my
trusted servants will overthrow Top
Muss and *I* will become the Muss
Leader. And *you* will become Master of
the entire Universe!"

Brandling let the idea sink in.

Dark Claw looked thoughtful.
"What about Onlee One?" he growled.

"Onlee One?" exclaimed Brandling.
"Oh, I have big plans for him.
He'll wish he'd never been born!"

"Excellent!" said Dark Claw. "I have plans for him, too. Perhaps we can make him suffer twice?"

"Ha! Ha! Ha!" Brandling, laughed nervously. She'd rather not know what Dark Claw had in mind for any Muss that crossed him.

"Very well," said Dark Claw. "Give your orders and commands, but never forget that I am your Master!"

He pressed a button on the control panel. He spoke into the console.

A Robo Kat's voice answered from the console. "Yes, Dark Claw… all space craft go to code green. Begin the invasion."

Dark Claw and Brandling stood by the window in the control room and watched as the massive fleet set its course for planet Muss.

Dark Claw spoke just loud enough for Brandling to hear. "I do not forgive failure."

Chapter 4

Brandling's old secretary, Ruse, approached Top Muss with his head bowed.

"I've had a message from Brandling," he said. "She's ordered me to have you locked up. Then she will return as our new leader."

Top Muss looked Ruse straight in the eye. "And are you going to follow her orders?" he asked.

"Of course n-n-not," stammered Ruse.

"Good!" Top Muss smiled.

They looked at a huge map that was covered in diagrams of Muss spaceships, but there was no sign of Dark Claw's fleet. Ruse explained to Top Muss how the Roboships didn't show up on Nosar.

The Roboships have smell repeaters on them that move the smell from behind them to in front of them. So our Nosars can't detect the Roboship fleet that is heading towards us.

Top Muss looked at the map. "Where do we think Dark Claw is coming from?" he asked.

Chin Chee pointed to the map with a stick. "Brandling went in this direction, so we think that's where Dark Claw will be coming from."

"Good," said Top Muss. "Send scout ships in that direction. We must find Dark Claw's fleet."

Onlee One looked at Hamee and Chin Chee. "Come on," he said.

That means Us!

Chapter 5

The voice of a Starpilot spilled across the radio. Another voice giggled.

"Language, please!" Onlee One spoke into his headset. "Have you anything to report?" he asked the scout pilots.

The Starpilot's excited voice crackled on the speakers.

I'm at position 29-34-52. It's incredible. There are hundred's... no! ...thousands of Roboships. I can see them but none of them show up on my Nosar.

Onlee One called into his headset. "Good work! Now get out of there!"

A moment later the panicked Starpilot came back on air. "I'm under attack! They're…" The radio crackled, then cut out. Every pilot listening knew what it meant.

Onlee One stayed calm. "Let's have a look at the starmap," he told Hammee and Chin Chee.

Chin Chee pointed out where Dark Claw's fleet should be. All three of them stared at the screen, trying to work out a plan. It looked hopeless.

Onlee One pointed to some dots on the screen that were heading towards Litterbox, the dirty brown moon that circled the Planet Muss. "What are those ships over there?" he asked.

Chin Chee checked their code numbers. "They're just trash barges."

Onlee One looked surprised. "Trash Barges!" he asked. "What do they do?"

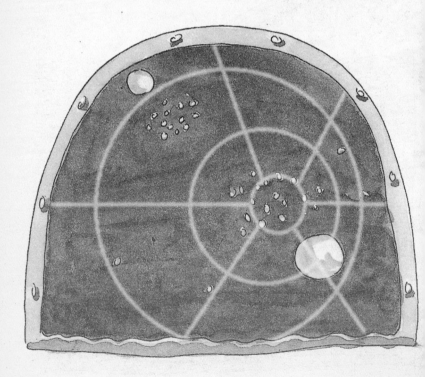

They transport all the waste from the Planet Muss to Litterbox," Chin Chee explained.

The waste is mushed up into a liquid and sprayed, so that the barges don't have to land on the revolting surface of Litterbox.

Onlee One nodded. A tiny idea flickered in his brain, and quickly developed into a plan.

"Right!" he called out. "Send the barges towards Dark Claw's fleet and spray them with trash. Then our Nosars will be able to smell them."

"That is such a crazy idea..." said Hammee

...it just might work!

Chapter 6

The trash barges were set on course.
As they closed in on their target,
millions of tons of toxic gloop was
sprayed at Dark Claw's armada.

The radios in a thousand Muss fighter craft sprang to life with chattering pilots.

"I've got them on the Nosar," said one.

They're showing up like Candle-trees. We can't miss them!

The Muss-guided missiles worked on smell, the same way Nosar did. Once they were locked onto that deep space stink, nothing could stop them reaching their targets.

There was no escape for the Robo Kat ships. One by one, they exploded into wildly coloured fireballs, as the missiles hit their gloop-covered targets.

Chapter 7

Dark Claw slammed down his fist. Slowly, he turned his burning yellow eyes towards Brandling.

"You have failed me!" he snarled.

"It's not my fault!" Brandling complained. "I was betrayed as well!"

Dark Claw and Brandling were racing back to the safety of Dark Moon. Dark Claw had watched his fleet explode around him. Now he ordered his surviving Roboships to retreat before they too were destroyed.

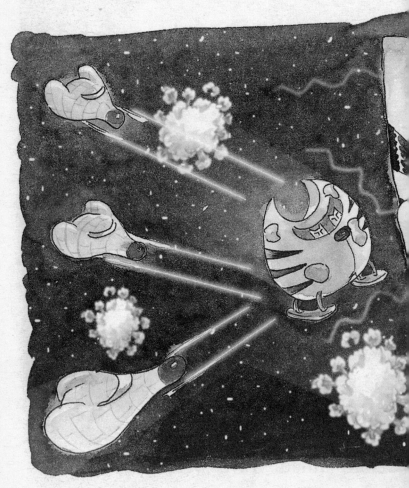

Meanwhile, Onlee One and the other Muss starpilots were on their tail.

"It's all Onlee One's fault!" Brandling whimpered.

Dark Claw froze at the sound of his arch-enemy's name and Brandling's blood ran cold. She had made a dreadful error!

Dark Claw held his paw in front of
Brandling's face. His one, dark claw
sprung out like a switchblade.

At the signal, two Robo Kat guards leapt forward and grabbed Brandling's arms.

Dark Claw prodded Brandling's chest. "No one fails me!" he hissed through gritted teeth.

No one!

Chapter 8

Dark Claw's ship entered the huge landing bay on Dark Moon. The giant space doors began closing behind it.

The Robo Kats marched Brandling to
the air-lock door and waited until it
was safe to leave the spaceship.

Brandling knew that Dark Claw meant
to put her to a slow, painful death, but
she wasn't going to let him get away
with it that easily.

Suddenly she lunged towards the airlock handle and grabbed it. The Robo Kats were too slow to stop her. She twisted the handle this way and that, until it clicked into the open position.

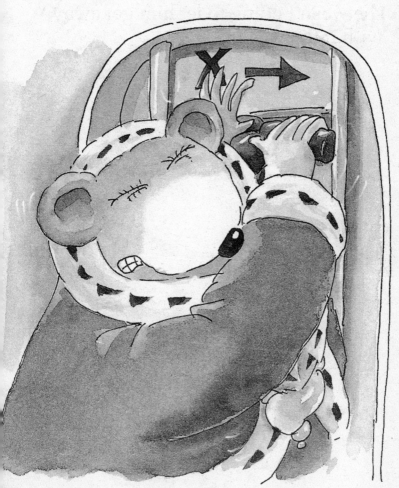

The air was filled with a piercing
screech as the door seals broke.
The screech turned into a roar as
air began to rush out of the ship.

The hanger doors weren't yet closed. They were still open to the vacuum of space. The vacuum pulled hungrily at the air lock door.

As Brandling felt the air being sucked from her lungs she managed one last laugh. She had beaten Dark Claw.

Then the door seal snapped against the immense pressure. The door smashed open and every last gasp of air blasted out of the ship and was lost into space.

Chapter 9

Onlee One, Chin Chee and Hammee parked outside Dark Moon. Nothing happened.

They knew Dark Claw was in there. Why didn't he shoot at them or something?

Chin Chee called over from the Nosar screen. "There's an alien craft coming this way. It says they come in peace."

A strange ship cruised up to Dark Moon's landing bay, and slipped through the gap where the space doors hadn't closed.

Onlee One felt the fur rise on the back of his neck. "Come on!" he said. "We're going in there too."

A minute later, they landed in the hanger bay. They put on their space suits, opened the air lock and walked down the ramp, to meet the crew of the other ship.

Two of the strangers walked towards them. The smaller one smiled at Onlee One. "You have done well, my son."

Onlee One turned to his friends. "This is my father, Pale One. And this is Spyra," he explained, pointing to the tall, beautiful Kat. "Dark Claw is her son."

Hammee and Chin Chee were speechless.

Spyra looked sad. "We have come to see our children," she said.

They followed her into Dark Claw's ship. Brandling's body lay by the door, still holding the lock.

"For once she did the right thing," Pale One said. "She sacrificed herself to save us all."

They found Dark Claw's body in the
control room. His one dark claw still
pointed from his velveted paw.

The two bodies were wrapped in gold cloth and sent out into space. Silently, side by side, they sped towards the great Black Hole.

Chapter 10

The war was over! On Planet Muss the celebrations lasted for days! Top Muss gave Hammee, Chin Chee and Onlee One the planet's highest honour for bravery.

Hammee ate and ate until he was his normal, cuddly self again.

Then the day came for Spyra and Pale One to return home.

"Look after Onlee One for me." Pale One asked Chin Chee.

Chin Chee smiled. "I will."

Onlee One did not know what to say to Spyra. After all, she had lost her only child in Dark Claw. But Spyra looked deep into his eyes and somehow he knew that words were not needed.

She held him close and whispered,

May the Guiding Paw be with you, Onlee One.

Chapter 11

Across the vast eternity of space, the bodies of Dark Claw and Brandling entered the singularity of the Great Black Hole, where the laws of nature are written and rewritten in the twinkling of an eye...

The end?

Have you seen the Dark Claw Website?

www.dark-claw.co.uk

Shoo Rayner designed and built the Dark Claw Website
himself, while he was writing the Dark Claw stories.
It is packed full of games and background stories about the
worlds of Onlee One, his friends and his enemies!

Why is Dark Claw so angry?
Why does he want to destroy the Muss?

 Where in the Universe is the planet Muss?
What is Litterbox? What is Kimono?

What is it like at the Tan Monastery School?
Why do the beds squeak?

All this and more. If you're a Dark Claw fan, you'll love the
Dark Claw website. It's all part of the story!

If you enjoyed this book you'll want to read the other books in the Dark Claw Saga.

Tunnel Mazers
0 340 81754 2
The one with the very
smelly cheese!

Road Rage
0 340 81755 0
The one with the cool
racing machines!

Rat Trap
0 340 81756 9
The one with invisible
space ships!

Breakout!
0 340 81757 7
The one with nowhere
left to go!

The Guiding Paw
0 340 81758 5
The one with the Muss-
eating jellyfish!

The Black Hole
0 340 81759 3
The one with the end
of the story!

Find out more about Shoo Rayner and his other
fantastic books at www.shoo-rayner.co.uk